# THE MAN I CALLED
# JOE JACKSON

# THE MAN I CALLED
# JOE JACKSON

JAMES WHITE

Printed in the United States of America By
One Communications LLC 800-621-2556

# CONTENTS

# ACKNOWLEDGMENTS

THE author wishes to express his gratitude to his brothers and sisters who contributed time and effort to ensure the completion of this book. He is indebted to his uncle, aunts, cousins, and friends who sent pictures and suggestions for his book.

# INTRODUCTION

MY name is Thomas Jackson. I was born the ninth day of June, 1846 in Richmond, Virginia. My mother's name is Carrie and my father is Master Tom Jackson. My mother told me that Master Tom was an overseer on the Johnson's plantation when he met Annie Johnson, the owner of the Johnson's plantation. After Miss Annie's husband, William Johnson Sr., died from smallpox in the summer of 1838, William Jr. sold most of the slaves to other plantation owners and eventually returned to Georgia, where he was a doctor and had his own family.

A year later Master Tom married Annie and had the remaining slaves continue to help her farm the fields of the plantation. Master Tom changed the name of the Johnson Plantation to the Jackson Plantation. At the time when Miss Annie married Master Tom, she was much older than him. The age of Mistress Annie—I was told that she was about sixty, and Master Tom was about forty.

During the first five years, Master Tom and Mistress had no children. Master Tom and Mistress owned about fifteen slaves before I was born. Over the years he bought more slaves to farm their five fields in Richmond. Master Tom was a good master to most of his slaves—especially to the young slave women. They bore him children to help run the plantation. Master Tom had several young house slaves who lived in the big house with him at all times to meet his personal needs. My mother was a house slave 'cause she had a very light complexion. Mother told me that old man Johnson was her father, and when he died he had asked Miss Annie in his will to not sell her to anyone unless she was losing all his money and his land. Miss promises me that they will not sell me and my family.

# SLAVE LIFE

THE story begins on the Johnson plantation in Richmond, Virginia, where my mother was a slave on the Johnson plantation. She was sold to Master Jackson from her old master's son for $500.00 at the age of fifteen. Master Tom told her old master, Annie's youngest son, William Jr., that one day she'd bear him children to help farm the land. During the summer of 1845 my mother was pregnant with my older brother, Joe, who was also very light-complected. All the slaves knew that Master Tom was the father, because Joe could past for a white baby. Joe was kept in the big house with Master Tom and Annie. Annie treated Joe as her own son and protected him from any other slaves, including our mother.

Mother told me that Master sold any slaves
who mentioned that Joe was not his wife's son.
During that year Tom sold five of his slaves,
leaving only ten to run the farm. Mother told
me the plantation needed about ten or more
slaves. She would see all the slaves walking by
the big house after a hard day's work. The only
time the slaves had off was Sunday morning
and Christmas. On Sunday the slaves would
gather together and have church near the
big house for several hours. After church the
slaves would go to the slaves' house and have
a big feast. They would eat until they got sick,
but the slaves would suffer the next day in the
fields, because they would work from sunrise
to sunset on Monday to Saturday. Master only
gave the slaves two breaks during the day.
Most of the older slaves would be so sick
at night that mother kept praying that God
would come and take them home with him.
The next year I was born, and I was dark-
complected. Mother and I stayed in the little
house behind the big house.

As the years passed, mother told me about

my brother and how we had to keep it a secret or we would be sold. Mother shared with me as I got older that the only man Master allowed her to talk to was him. If he caught any other man talking to her outside the big house, he would be sold. By the time I was five, Master Tom had fathered ten other children by his slaves. Most of the slave's children were Master Tom's because his old wife could not bear any of her own. Somehow word got out to other plantations that the old mistress was too old to bear the five children that she was calling her own children without having any of them herself.

During the fall of 1851 Master Tom and Mistress were tired of the nearby plantations talking about the children, so Master Tom and Mistress sold their plantation and moved me, Mommy (who was expecting another baby), and the other five light-skinned children to South Carolina, where Master Tom had a brother and a good friend. He also sold all of the other slaves—including his other dark-skinned children—to nearby plantations in Virginia. He only took me along because of the will that Annie's first husband had left, and Mommy said that he would kill her if she had to leave me. So Mistress told Master to take both of us along, and he did.

# RELOCATION

WE arrived on James Island on September 6, 1851. It took us a month to get there. The new plantation that Master Tom and Mistress Annie had bought was very large; it was about three hundred acres of clear land that we had to farm each year. We had a big house with no slaves' quarters. Master told mother, "Since you brought your dark son, you have to sleep outside with him until the slave quarters get built. Joe and the other children stayed in the house, because neighbors thought that they were white.

Master Tom went to town and brought back twenty slaves to build slave houses for us to live in and to work the plantation. When they got back, Master Tom helped the slaves build the quarters. Mistress would make lemonade and cookies for lunch while everyone helped build the quarters. The children would help with carrying wood and mixing the clay and straw. After about two weeks the ten slaves' quarters were built. Our houses had two rooms each; the big house had nine rooms. Each quarter had a fireplace, bedroom, and one window. Each house could only hold about four people.

Joe and my new baby brother, Jack, were well-mannered and liked by anyone they met. As we grew up, Joe and Jack would teach me the proper language and how to read when Master Tom wasn't around. We had a good relationship because Mother told them that we must take care of one other, in case someone found out they were nigger. Joe told Mother that he and Jack would be very careful to not allow any white person to know that their mother was not Mistress Annie.

Mistress was a different person on James Island. She was a lot of fun. She played games with everyone, treated everyone fairly, give the slaves their own land to farm and allowed them to sell their produce. Mistress taught all the slaves to read and write. She even gave mother permission to interact with other male slaves and let her become a real mother figure to Joe and Jack. Times were getting better for the slaves. Every summer Master and Mistress would go to the inner city of Charleston for the summer because of diseases and hot weather. Most of the summer Mother and I stayed in the big house with the other children until the fall. Then we had to move back to the slave quarters. But we enjoyed living like a family with Joe, Jack, and the other kids.

Mistress was get older, and she told mother that she was trying to get herself right with God. Every Sunday she allowed Rev. Davis to have a service on the plantation for all the slaves. During that day everyone was treated the same, and after the service we would have a big dinner at the big house.

# CHANGES

YEARS went by, and everyone was talking about South Carolina leaving the Union. Other states said that they might follow South Carolina if they wanted to start their own government. I was told that it was because the North wanted to end slavery and the South wanted to continue to use slaves on the plantations.

After moving to James Island we had plenty to eat: beef, pork, collard, peas, cornbread, fruit, milk, and rice. Mother cooked biscuits and made butter once a week. Every time Mother cooked I would watch her, then she started teaching me how to cook. Mother

said that I was a fast learner, so I started to
cook food for everyone during the holidays
and on Sundays.

In 1858 Master and Mistress did not leave
for the summer because Mistress was too
ill to leave the house. That was the summer
when Annie Jackson died of natural causes.
Master Tom stayed in the big house all day
with the Rev. Davis as visitors came by. That
was one of the saddest days on the   plantation, because everyone loved Mistress Annie.

She was very caring to all the slaves. She
would not let Master Tom touch or beat any
slaves after we had moved to South Carolina.
Each summer we would go to Charleston to
sell our corn, beans, and other crops to save
money to buy our freedom. Before Mistress
died she said that when we got $100.00
mother could buy our freedom, but she died
too soon, 'cause Mother had about $80.00. I
knew that Master would not sell our freedom
'cause it was a secret between Mistress and
Mother, and Master would not agree to it.

A week after Mistress died Master Tom

went to Charleston and stayed the rest of the summer. He came back and started talking about how South Carolina and other states had seceded from the Union, and would be called the Confederate States. Master said that the United States government was upset with the states that had left and was asking them to change their minds, because the president wanted to keep the Union together. The United States government told the seceding states that it would do anything to save the Union—even fight a war.

Master said if a war broke out he would ask the slaves to help protect the plantation. Most of the slaves agreed to do whatever it took to help our master. Everyone agreed that he was a good man, and the mistress would have asked the same.

On April 12, 1861, we heard a loud *boom*, *boom* early that morning. We went outside, and everyone was cheering, saying that the Confederates had opened fire with fifty cannons upon Fort Sumter in Charleston, South Carolina. The Civil War had begun.

# HELPING THE SOUTH

AFTER we got dressed, most of the slaves and freemen of Charleston and on the island wanted to help the south. We went to the enlistment station to join, but all of us were turned down as soldiers; they wanted to use us for laborers. The Confederates said it would be over soon, and it was a white man war. So most of the slaves returned to their plantations and helped their masters prepare for war.

Rumor was that President Lincoln was asking men to volunteer for his army. Some of the slaves started to move up north so they could join with the Union army. The next day Joe and I went to Charleston and joined the 6th South Carolina Volunteers—all-white unit. Since everyone thought Joe was white, he enlisted as a soldier. They asked me to be a cook for the unit, since no black could serve as a soldier. One of the soldiers told Joe that they had been present at the bombardment of Fort Sumter.

Jack was in Charleston helping Master Tom, but that evening Joe and I said good-bye to Mother and our friends, and we headed down south. After we said good-bye we marched to recruit more members. We went to every small town and big city recruiting soldiers. By the time we arrived in Georgia we had over five hundred men in our unit. Gen. John Bratton, who commanded the unit, was dividing soldiers into companies. Joe was in Company C. His company had one hundred soldiers from all over South Carolina. My duties in the 6th South Carolina were to gather wood for cook fires, polish metal fittings, groom, feed, and water horses, clear fields for parades and drills, and do water details for the cook house.

At the camp I read a newspaper while in the tent with others cooks. I had to keep it a secret that I could read and write. Only Joe knew. Most of the white soldiers in the regiment could not read or write, and if they found out that I knew how to read and write they would harm me or even kill me. The newspaper was stating that President Abraham Lincoln had trouble deciding whether to recruit black soldiers. Eleven slave states had already left, or seceded from, the United States. There were four more states that allowed slavery. Some of the soldiers said that Lincoln was afraid that if he allowed black men to fight, thereby emancipating them, those last four slave states would secede, too. Lincoln hoped that the war could be won quickly without using African American soldiers. The newspaper said the Confederates had won several battles, such as

Bull Run in Virginia, and Wilson's Creek in southwest Missouri. Many soldiers from both sides were being killed and wounded. But still, neither the North nor the South would allow black soldiers to fight, because they thought the war would be over soon. Some officers in camp thought African Americans should be part of the Confederate navy.

While I was helping the Confederates, the officer let me gather the food and serve hot meals to the soldiers at camp. The average Confederate subsisted on bacon, cornmeal, molasses, peas, vegetables, and rice. Soldiers also received a coffee substitute, which was not as desirable as the real coffee.

The Southern soldier was highly regarded for traveling with a very light load—basically because he did not have the extra items available to him that the Northern soldier had. The Southern uniforms were quite different from the Northern uniforms, consisting of a short-waist jacket and trousers made of "jean" cloth—a blend of wool and cotton threads that was very durable. The uniforms were a variation of grays and browns. Some of Northern soldiers on the battle field called Confederates "butternuts" because of the tan-grey color of the uniforms. Vests were also worn and were often made of jean material as well. Of course there were shirts and undergarments too.

During the months with the 6th South Carolina I saw not one Northern soldier except for the dead ones on the battlefields. Most of the time, I was used to assist with injuries or to help bury the dead after the battles. I didn't see Joe until after the battles, and he would make sure I saw him when he arrived back at camp. Joe and I could only talk for two minutes every day to keep up our spirits. Most of the soldier was calling all the black help nigger or boy.

Joe and I were the only ones who knew how to read, but only Joe knew that I knew how to read, and he knew not to tell anybody. Since Joe knew how to read and write, he was promoted to first sergeant about two weeks after he enlisted. Joe said that he didn't like to tell the soldiers what and what not to do. He would always ask the soldiers to be nice to the blacks helping them.

# Helping the North

WHEN we arrived back in Columbia, South Carolina in July, I talked to Joe about joining the North army so we could fight side-by-side when they would recruit blacks. We got news that Lincoln opposed early efforts to recruit black soldiers, even though he accepted their use as laborers. Joe said that he had promised his father that he would help the South win the war.

At this point I told Joe that I was going to join the Union army, and he started crying, saying that I couldn't because we had promised Dad that we would support the South. I was going to join an all-colored regiment to fight for the North, anyway. Later that night I left camp to join a local Union regiment on James Island, South Carolina. The Regiment was called the First South Carolina Colored Infantry Volunteers. When I joined that unit in 1862 there were thousands of young Americans who left homes to fight for their causes; it was an experience that we would never forget. Being with the First South Carolina Volunteers meant many months away from Joe and love ones, long hours of drills during most days, and days spent marching on hot, dusty roads or in a rain and snow.

I received our uniform about three months after I joined. Our uniform was red pants and blue jacket. But they were not quite as fancy as those worn by the hometown militias. Several months later the unit received our guns and the Manual of Arms and other procedures about muskets. I lived in rectangular piece of canvas buttoned to another to form a small two-man tent, or dog tent, as the soldiers called them. I would crawl under it and stay dry from the rain. The tent could be easily pitched for the evening by tying each end to a rifle stuck in the ground by the bayonet or by stringing it up to fence rails.

We did drills and covered picket duties for most of the winter. During our free time we played cards and talked around the fire pit. After the festive New Year's Day celebration, we left our camp to go into the field from January 23 to February 1, 1863. We were on expedition from Beaufort up the St. Mary's River, which is between Georgia and Florida. I was cold and hungry most of the time. We did not have a lot to eat—only a small amount. Every three days they gave each soldier a ration of rice, dry meat, and hardtack, which had to last three days.

Our goal while in the field was to surprise a Confederate encampment and capture much-needed lumber stores. A skirmish developed as we were intercepted by a Confederate patrol before reaching the encampment. We lost several men; all of them were good friends of mine. After the skirmish we buried the men and headed toward camp. This skirmish was the first hand-to-hand combat for the regiment. I was very scared. I had never been that close to where soldiers were dying all around me. With the Confederates, we had stayed at the back and helped at the camp hospital, so I had never been close to the fighting.

That night I wrote back home to tell mother that I was okay. I had not heard from mother since Joe and I had left about two years earlier. I hoped that Jack was still home to take care of Mother. He said that he would not join any army—that he would take care of Mother and the farm.

My captain told me that we would be marching to Jacksonville, Florida the next day. It was about six o clock, and everyone was going to bed so they wouldn't be tired while marching. At 5:00 AM we got our morning call. After breakfast we started marching to Jacksonville. We marched for four months and several days before arriving in Jacksonville. We were in another skirmish. This time we were prepared. We killed more soldiers than we lost.

When arriving in Jacksonville, I received a letter from Jack saying that mother had died from worrying about a year ago. He said that

he had tried to get in touch with me and Joe,
but no one knew how to contact us. Also, he
received a letter from Joe last year that Joe
had been shot at the Battle of Bull Run and
was in a hospital somewhere up north. Jack
said that the Union army was using the big
house for a hospital.

After staying in Jacksonville for months
during picket duty, we left to head back to
South Carolina in November. On the way
back we ran into a group of Confederates just
before arriving in Hilton Head. Again we lost
some men, but we ran the Confederates out of
Hilton Head. On May 22, 1863, we heard that
The United States War Department had issued
General Order Number 143 establishing a
"Bureau of Colored Troops" to facilitate the
recruitment of African-American soldiers
to fight for the Union army. Regiments,
including infantry, cavalry, light-artillery units,
and heavy-artillery units were recruited from
all states of the Union, and became known
as the United States Colored Troops (USCT).

The regiment changed its name from the 1st South Carolina to the 33rd United States Colored Infantry on the 8th of February. We got to wear blue wool pants with our uniforms instead of the red ones; a belt set that included a cartridge box, cap box, bayonet, and scabbard; a haversack for rations; a canteen; and a blanket roll or knapsack, which contained a wool blanket, a shelter half, and perhaps a rubber blanket or poncho. Inside was a change of socks, writing paper, stamps, envelopes, ink and pen, razor, toothbrush, comb, and other personal items. The amount of baggage each soldier carried differed from man to man.

Drums were used in the infantry to announce daily activities from sunrise to sunset. Reveille was sounded to begin the day at 5:00 AM, followed by an assembly for morning roll call and breakfast call. Sick call was sounded soon after breakfast, followed by assemblies for guard duty, drill, or to begin the march. Drummers were also important on the march to keep soldiers in step during parades and to call them to attention. In battle, drums were sometimes used to signal maneuvers and give signals for the ranks to load and fire their weapons. We were told that a soldier's pay was thirteen dollars per month, but instead we received only a laborer's pay, thus serving for six dollars a month less than did white soldiers.

Free time was spent in card games, reading, pitching horseshoes, or team sports, such as the fledgling sport of baseball, a game that rapidly gained favor among the troops. Rule booklets were widely distributed, and the game soon became a favorite. We also played a form of football that appeared more like a huge brawl than the game.

In June of 1864, the regiment was ordered to Folly Island until after the siege of Charleston. We participated in the battle of Honey Hill and the capture of a fort on James Island, where Confederates sustained casualties. During my last year of service, from February 1865 to February 1866, the regiment was employed in provost and picket duty in Charleston. Our last day as a regiment was at Fort Wagner on February 9, 1866. On that day I left the army with my uniform and fifteen dollars in my pocket. Several of my friends were from James Island, so we decided to leave the next day to head back home.

# AFTER THE WAR

ON February 10, we started walking back to James Island, hoping to see everybody that we had not seen during the war. I returned to the Jackson Plantation in several days and saw that all of the slave houses were still standing, but the big house had been burned to the ground. That day I saw Rev. Davis. He told me that Jack and the other slaves had been killed protecting the farm after the war had ended. Rev. Davis said when the soldiers heard the news that the war was over, they started taking everything from the big house and then started burning everything that they could not carry with them. All the slaves, including Jack, were killed trying to stop the soldiers from burning the house. When the slaves had started walking toward the soldiers the soldiers had started shooting and killing them. They did not stop shooting until everyone was dead, and then they started marching off. I started crying and Rev. Davis asked me to stop; he said, "They are in a better place now."

He led me to the place where he had buried them a few feet behind the slave houses. Jack was buried beside mother and several feet from Master and Annie. That evening two of my war friends came over to see the plantation and to head north. I told them what Rev. Davis had told me, and then I asked them to stay for the night 'cause it was getting late. They said that they had no place to go. Their old master would not allow them to come back on the plantation. I gave each one a slave house for the night, and I told them that because the plantation was so big I would give them each a piece of land to build a house on and enough to have small farm.

The next day I gave my friends the land, and we started to rebuild our live as *freemen*. During the next several months we had two houses built—each one with three bedrooms, a kitchen, and a fireplace in the sitting area. The last house we built was mine. I wanted a large one with four bedrooms.

Two years passed with no word from Joe. I was told by a soldier that he had died in a hospital several months before the war had ended. I had become a minster and married Mary Davis. She is Rev. Davis's youngest daughter, who is three years younger than me. We have one son who I named Jack. My two friends are doing very well also; John and David are married to sisters from an old plantation nearby.

Other years passed. One morning I was in the field when Mary came up to me and said that someone wanted to see me at the house. I left the field and headed back toward the house, seeing a man in the distance wearing a dark suit. As I approached the house he started to cry, calling my name. I knew it was Joe. My heart started pounding about Mother and Jack. I told him what Rev. Davis had told me. We both started to cry. It was one of my happiest moments that I'd had in a long time.

During the next five years Joe became a businessman and married a local lady from James Island, named Beth. They had three sons and one daughter. Our families continue to keep in touch daily and farm together each year. Joe lived to be seventy-eight years old. He died from natural causes a year after Beth died. His children still live in South Carolina. His youngest son lives on the old plantation beside me. I continue to minster to the people. My wife, Mary, died last year. My only son and his family live with me on the old plantation. David and John both died a few years ago from heart problems.

# EPILOGUE

O N July 4 1890, Thomas Jackson died in his sleep. His son, Jack, was by his side. Approximately 175 regiments of over 200,000 free blacks and freed slaves served during the last two years of the war, bolstering the Union war effort. By war's end, the USCT were approximately a tenth of all Union troops. USCT regiments were led by white officers. USCT were also placed in their own brigades. In the Army of the James, black troops made up Brigadier General William Birney's Colored Brigade of the X Corps. Brigadier General Charles J. Paine's 3rd Division of the XVIII Corps was made up of three all-USCT brigades: the 1st Brigade led by Colonel John Holman, the 2nd Brigade commanded by Colonel Alonzo G. Draper, and Colonel Samuel Duncan's 3rd Brigade.

CHICAGO HISTORICAL SOCIETY